OOPSY❀DAISY'S
BAD BAD DAY

by Brian Brooks
for Cosmic Debris

CHRONICLE BOOKS
SAN FRANCISCO

www.oopsy-daisy.com

Library of Congress Cataloging-in-Publication Data available.

ISBN 0-8118-3539-1   10 9 8 7 6 5 4 3 2 1

Manufactured in Singapore
Distributed in Canada by
Raincoast Books
9050 Shaughnessy Street
Vancouver, B.C. V6P 6E5

Chronicle Books LLC
85 Second Street
San Francisco, Calif. 94105
www.chroniclebooks.com

Dedicated to everybody who has Bad Bad Days.
If you don't ever have Bad Bad Days, well, this is for you, too.
Special thanks to Noël Tolentino, and Robert Reger.
To my Mom and Family, the People Upstairs,
the Cosmic Crew, Fashion Colt, Beat Angels,
Jonathan Richman, Nick Lowe,
and George Harrison.

HELP ME?

One fine day, Oopsy **awoke!**

As usual, she got
up on the wrong
side of the bed.

I'VE GOT A FUNNY FEELING ABOUT TODAY.

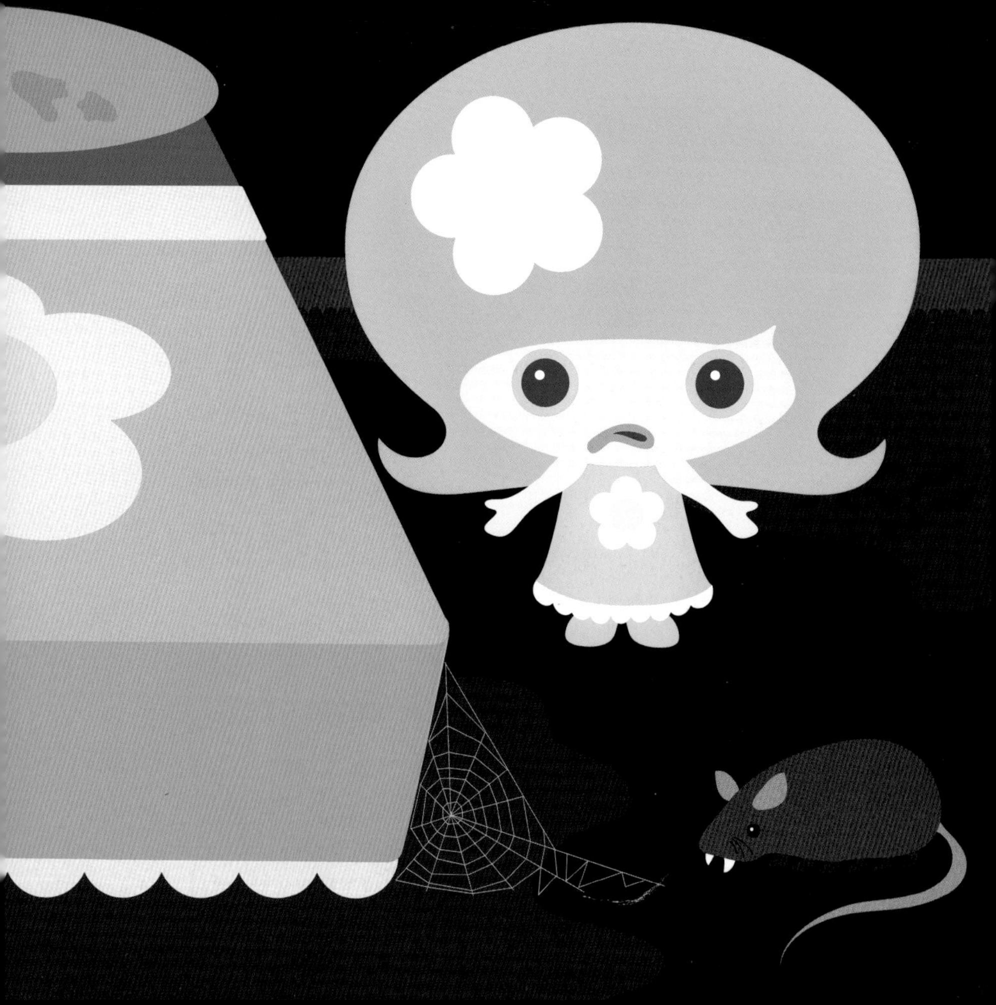

The bath overflowed,
the toothpaste attacked!

The mirror made a funny face.

OOPSY O'S
AND OTHER LETTERS

Did you know that eating Oopsy O's was actually bad for you? That's right! Eating just one bowl of Oopsy O's is like eating a lion, a tiger, and a bear! Oh my! So why not try something natural that won't rot your teeth, make you silly, and keep you uncontrollably hyper??? Because Oopsy O's are fun, that's why! And it's fun to have fun... Or my name isn't Oopsy Daisy.

Oopsy Daisy

YOU ARE DUMB.

NOW MORE MEAN

Net Wt. wiz of OZ

Even her cereal was mean!

Oopsy ran for the door, but she missed!

**Outside was topsy turvy,
Oopsy Daisy was upsy downsy!**

Oopsy heard sirens in the distance, so she ran.

stay off the grass

OUCHY,
THE ZOO
HURTS!

Oopsy Daisy rolled downtown.

The business people were angry.

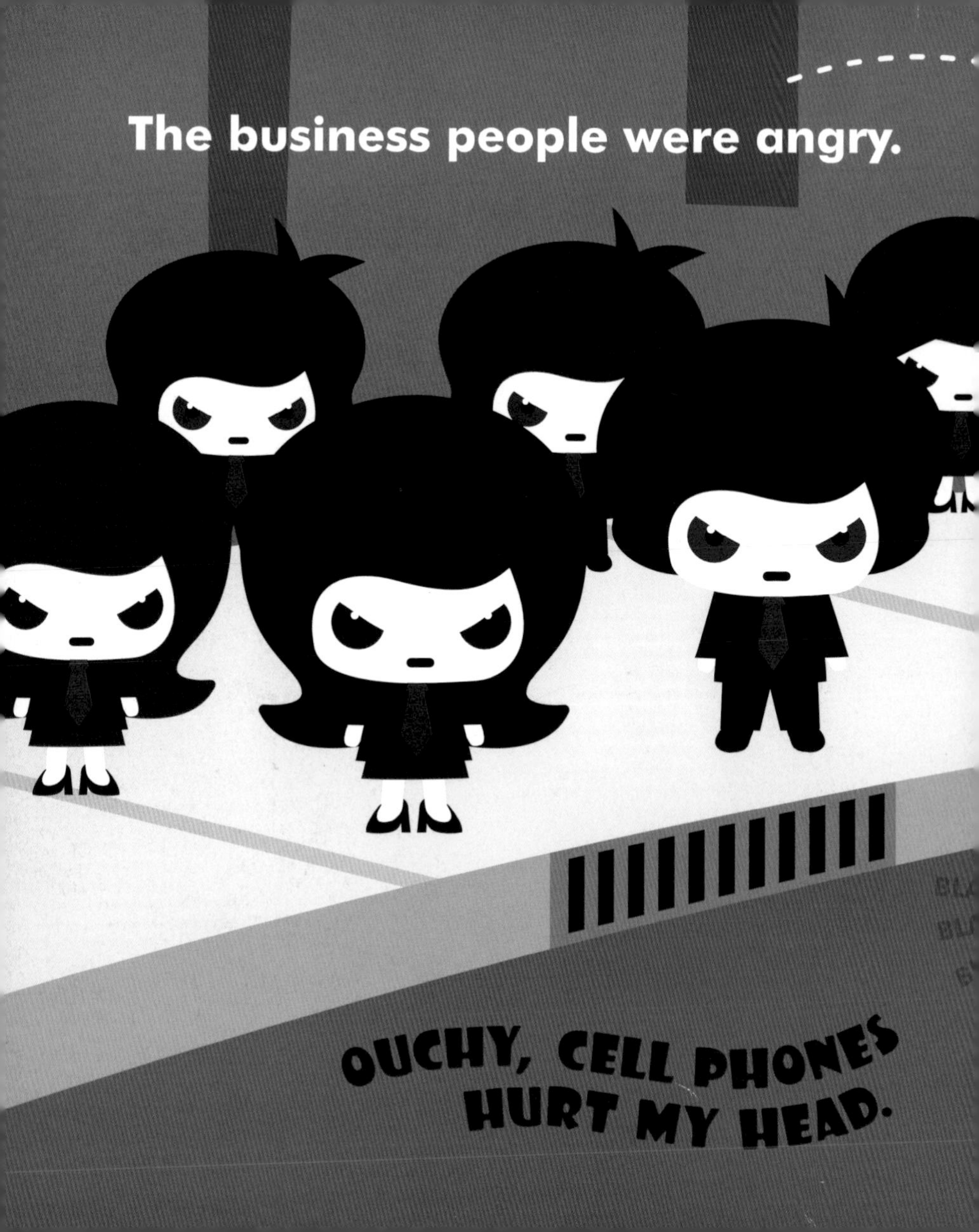

Without warning, ninjas attacked...
from the sky!

OOPS, I KILLED A
GANG OF NINJAS!

DON'T TOUCH

START

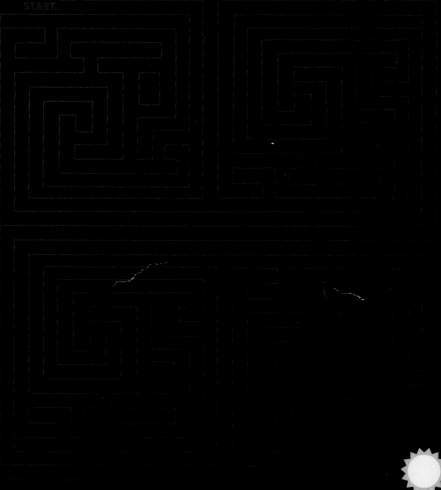

All of the Special Friends were there.

HELLO, FRIENDS!

WHY IS EVERYBODY CHEERING?
DID I WIN AN AWARD?

All of a sudden,
Oopsy had a funny feeling...

She was in for a bad bad night.

She was right.